A Little Time

Ginny had just moved next door, and I liked her right away. We got to be friends and I invited her to come home with me after school. We ran into the house and threw down our things. Then Ginny saw Matt.

"What's wrong with him?" Ginny asked in a funny voice.

"He's mongoloid," I told her.

"What's that?"

"It's also called Down's syndrome. Something happened before he was born," I explained. "It isn't his fault. He has too many chromosomes."

Ginny didn't say anything.

"Listen," I said, "making a baby's very complicated. Lots of different things can go wrong. But it doesn't usually happen. Most babies come out fine. It's a kind of miracle."

I was repeating what Mama had told me, trying to convince myself. . . .

Sarah loves Matt, her younger brother, but she sometimes wishes he weren't around to spoil things, and when her mother can't come to the special Mother-Daughter Day at school, when her birthday party is almost ruined, when Ginny starts a private club that excludes her—and all because of Matt—it is almost too much to bear. Yet the alternative —sending Matt away—seems intolerable too.

In *A Little Time* Anne Norris Baldwin sympathetically explores the interaction of parents, children, friends, and community and depicts with warmth and deep feeling the difficulties and rewards of growing up with a mongoloid child. ✍

A
Little Time

Anne Norris Baldwin

The Viking Press
New York

First published in 1978 by The Viking Press
625 Madison Avenue, New York, N.Y. 10022
Published simultaneously in Canada by
Penguin Books Canada Limited
Printed in U.S.A.
2   3   4   5   82   81   80   79

Library of Congress Cataloging in Publication Data
Baldwin, Anne Norris.   A little time.
Summary: A ten-year-old begins to understand
her feelings and those of her family toward her younger
brother who has Down's syndrome.
[1. Down's syndrome—Fiction. 2. Mentally
handicapped—Fiction] I. Title.
PZ7.B1819Li   [Fic]   77-27764
ISBN 0-670-43392-6

∾ For the friends who have taught me about our common humanity through their compassion for handicapped children

A Little Time

1

Matt, my brother, is different from other children. He is four years old, two years older than Peter, but Peter already walks better and says short sentences. Matt walks in jerks, sometimes very fast, but always clumsily, as if his stubby arms and legs were made of wood.

Suddenly, for no reason, he sits down—*plop*. It doesn't hurt him. He is round, like a beach ball. His sit-down place is still padded with diapers that make him look even rounder than he really is. He looks up at me with his soft blue eyes, and he smiles all over his face. He garbles sounds, moving his mouth around them, tasting them, without quite shaping them into words.

His face is a full-moon face, and his smile covers all of it. His eyes don't look deep into me. Even when he wants something, they are misty, as if he were seeing something far, far away. His smile is completely trusting. I put my arms around him, under his armpits, and lift him onto his feet again.

He is heavy, and I almost lose my balance. "Leave Mattie alone," Janet says. "He doesn't want to be dragged around like that."

Janet is fifteen, the oldest of the five children in our family. Next comes Mary, who's twelve; then me, Sarah, ten; then Matt and Peter.

Janet is wrong about Matt. He smiles past me and toddles toward a spot of color he has seen—perhaps the flowered cover of the armchair or the yellow lamp shade. Sometimes I think I am the only one who really understands Mattie.

When Mom is too busy to watch Matt, she puts him in a playpen. Peter can climb out of the playpen; he has hardly ever been in it. But Matt sits for a long time with his fingers curled through the string net. I am sorry he has to sit there, caged that way. I know he minds, because when we let him out, he runs all over, as fast as he can.

I give him a stuffed animal or a rubber ball. He throws it out of the pen right away. I give it back, and he throws it again. It is his favorite game. He chortles happily. Over and over again he throws the toy, until I say, "That's all now, Mattie." Then he reaches out and slaps my hand to tell me I am bad. He wants me to go on playing.

"One more time," I tell him. "Then that's all."

He laughs again as I hand him the toy. He is like Mary's puppy. He wants attention all the time.

Sometimes I mind Matt. Sometimes I get angry at him. But I don't resent him the way I did before he went away. I minded him a lot then. You see, I wanted to be friends with Ginny, and Matt got in the way.

Ginny had just moved here, and I liked her right away. She had long blond hair and a pretty face. After my teacher, Miss Williams, introduced her, Ginny kept glancing all around the class. The rest of us had started school two weeks earlier, so we all knew each other already. I knew Ginny felt shy and uncertain, because I had felt that way when we moved here from Ohio two years before.

I remembered how lonely I was in California at first. I didn't like anything! I thought the brown hills were ugly, and the trees all looked too short. I missed the deep blue Ohio sky, with its puffy clouds, and the tall elm tree in front of our two-story white house. I missed thunderstorms and the fall colors and snow, but most of all, I missed Connie, my best, best friend. Connie had lived on our street, and we were always together. The day we left forever, I cried all the way to Chicago, because I was sure I would never have another friend like Connie.

The way Ginny walked and held her head reminded me of Connie. "Where are you from?" I asked her at recess that first day. I knew she wasn't from San Jose.

"Connecticut," she replied eagerly. She tossed her hair back and smiled.

"I used to live near Cleveland," I told her. "We

6

moved here when my Dad got a new job."

"Same with us," she said. "My father's an engineer," she added proudly. "He designs airplane parts. He was promoted to Director of Research."

"My dad's a salesman for an electronics company," I told her. "He travels a lot. Mom doesn't like that part, but he makes more money now, and there's a good school for Matt here in San Jose."

"Who's Matt?" Ginny asked.

"My brother," I said. "He goes to a special school."

Ginny looked puzzled, but I didn't know her well enough to explain more. Some people understood about Matt right away, and others never did. I studied Ginny's face, but I couldn't tell which type she would be. With Connie, it had been easy: she had been my friend even before Matt was born.

I showed Ginny around the school, and we ate lunch together on a bench outside. We talked about how different California is from the East. "Green isn't really green, and blue isn't really blue," Ginny complained. "The hills and the sky all look the same." Ginny was the first person I had met out here who understood all that!

7

A week later she invited me to spend Saturday with her. Mom drove me out to her house, since it was too far to walk. I thought her house was beautiful! She was an only child, yet her house was even bigger than ours. It had a swimming pool and an enormous old oak tree. I was surprised, because Ginny didn't seem spoiled. She always asked *me* what I wanted to play at recess, yet she had bunk beds in her room just to have friends sleep over! Mary and I have bunk beds, but that's because our room is small.

We swam all morning, and after lunch Ginny's mother took us to a fair. She bought us balloons and cotton candy, and we went on all the rides. It was wonderful!

On the way home Ginny said, "I thought when we moved here I wouldn't have any friends." That was how I knew I meant more to her than just someone to take to the fair.

I was very excited and happy and invited her to come home from school with me the next Tuesday. Then I worried about it for a whole day. We didn't have any swimming pool, and our house was very crowded compared to hers, but mostly it was Matt. I knew I should warn Ginny about him, but I didn't know how.

On Tuesday we went home together on the bus. We ran into the house and threw down our things on the couch. "Hi, Mom, we're home," I called out. "Ginny's here."

Mom came down the hall from the bedrooms and greeted Ginny. She offered us a snack, and we ate some strawberry yogurt at the kitchen table. I knew Matt would get up from his nap soon. I tried not to think about it, but suddenly I couldn't eat my yogurt. I gave the rest to Peter, who had climbed up on the seat beside me and was trying to stick his fingers into my bowl.

After Ginny had finished eating, we wandered out into the patio. Our back yard probably looked very small to Ginny, but it has a nice old apricot tree. I showed her my doll carriage that happened to have been left near the picnic table, and then we played with Mary's puppy, who is all wiggly and soft.

All the time, I was listening for Matt. At last I heard his quick, loud footsteps on the hall floor. "Let's play a game," Ginny was just saying. "What games do you have?" She turned toward the house and pushed back the sliding glass door.

Then Ginny saw Matt. He was sitting on the floor about three feet inside the door, where she couldn't miss him. He rocked back and forth, back and forth. He was gurgling and drooling, and his diapers smelled: Mom hadn't changed him yet since his nap. His tongue hung out of his mouth.

Ginny froze. I walked over to Matt and ruffled his hair. He smiled his big smile at me, and then his eyes found Ginny. He whirled around and swung his arm at her. She jumped back, startled. He laughed in his funny way, and his eyes looked for her again, but she had backed off. She looked terribly frightened.

"He just wants to make friends," I said lamely. "Come on. Let's go down to my room."

"What's *wrong* with him?" Ginny asked in a funny voice.

"He's mongoloid," I told her.

"What's that?"

"Something happened before he was born," I explained. "It isn't his fault. He has too many chromosomes. No one knows why."

10

Ginny didn't say anything. She didn't even ask me what chromosomes are. She just turned all queer and silent.

"Listen," I said pleadingly, "making a baby's very complicated. Lots of different things can go wrong."

"I hope I never have any babies, then," Ginny said.

"But it doesn't usually happen. Most babies come out fine. That's the amazing thing. It's a kind of miracle."

I was repeating what Mom had told me, trying to convince myself as much as Ginny. Ginny nodded, but something had gone all wrong. When we went back to the living room, she kept glancing sideways at Matt, and that scared look came back into her face. I couldn't keep her attention. She didn't feel like playing any of the games I had, after all. We ended up just watching television all afternoon, although there wasn't any good show on. At last she went home, and I kicked a ball around outside until Dad came home and supper was ready.

"You're very quiet tonight, Sarah," Dad said. "Did you have a bad day at school?"

"No," I said. I didn't want to talk about Ginny.

After supper I lay down on the living-room floor to draw a picture. It was a lovely picture, with flowers and birds and a house—our house. Just as I finished it, Matt came along and stamped right on it. "Mattie, get off!" I cried out. "You've wrecked my picture. See, it's torn now." I shoved Matt away. He sat down, looking puzzled.

Dad said, "Don't be so rough, Sarah. You know Matt doesn't understand."

"But he wrecked my picture. It was for you."

"Come here," Dad said gently. He motioned with his hand.

"I don't feel like it."

He shrugged. "All right, then. I know how you feel."

Then tears boiled up inside me. I squeezed in beside Dad in the big armchair, where he always sits when he reads his newspaper, and I traced the flower pattern on the arm of the chair with my finger.

"Sarah," Dad said slowly, "all of us who have everything we were meant to have are very, very fortunate."

"I know all that," I sobbed, "but Matt never gets

blamed for anything. Even the things he does on purpose. It isn't fair."

"I suppose that's true."

"Then *why*?"

"How can I answer that?" he said in a tired voice. "*Life* isn't fair, that's all. If you talk about fairness, it's Matt who has the least. We're the rich ones, so we can afford to be kind. Make me another picture. I'd like that very much."

When I finished it, he said, "That's very nice." He held it up and studied it carefully. "What kind of flower's that?"

"An oleander bush."

"That's a new touch. I like that."

"And that's our apricot tree."

"This picture's better," he said. "It has more in it. Now just think. If Matt hadn't torn your first one, you wouldn't have made this."

I felt better then, so I gave Matt the first one, and he crumpled it all up and laughed.

"Silly!" I told him. "That's not what pictures are for!"

I caught Dad's eye, and it was a little joke between us.

~2

I avoided Ginny all week. I didn't know what to say to her any more. It made me very unhappy. Her seat was in the same row as mine, several desks away. I watched her and wondered if she was unhappy too. While she was reading, she pushed her hair behind her ear, and her head tilted to the side. She didn't ever look my way.

Peter had a cold and Mom caught it from him. "I don't know what happened," she said. "I never get sick.

I don't have time. I just hope Matt won't catch it. His colds go on forever."

She was getting him dressed for school, and he was giggling and tugging at his shirt.

"What's so funny, Matt?"

"You put his shirt on backwards!" Mary exclaimed.

"So I did!"

We all laughed then. "Mattie's smarter than you are, Mom!" I teased her. "*He* knew it was on backwards."

"He *did*, didn't he? Oh, Matt, that's wonderful!" She pulled the shirt over his arms and turned it around. She showed him how to put his arms back through the sleeves, and he tried very hard to do it, but his hand caught. "Al *most*, Mattie," Mom said. "You almost have it. Someday you'll be able to get dressed all by yourself." Her eyes glistened with tears.

"Why are you crying?" I asked her.

"It gives me such hope when he learns something new. Each little thing means so much. Do you remember learning to tie your shoes?" she asked me as she pulled a shoe onto Matt's foot and quickly double-tied it.

"No."

"You wouldn't let anyone help. It took forever. Every time we went out, I had to allow an extra half hour."

"How silly."

"No—learning that was a big achievement. We forget. We take so much for granted. With Matt we can't. He makes me live slowly enough to feel every step. That's the gift of joy he brings." She set him on his feet and kissed his cheek.

"He doesn't make *me* too awfully joyful," I mumbled so that Mom could barely hear.

She straightened up and looked at me thoughtfully. "Was it Ginny?" she asked pointedly.

Startled, I nodded, and then had to struggle to keep tears out of my eyes.

"She'll get used to him," Mom said gently. We were both silent for a moment. Mom tucked her shirttail into her slacks and picked a sweat shirt up off the floor while I stood there. She went on. "You know, it's frightening to people at first when they see a handicapped child. They see he's different, and they don't know what he might do. We have to give them time to realize he won't hurt them. It's better if you prepare people first. Then they aren't scared."

I nodded and began looking for my schoolbooks, but I didn't feel any better. It was too late now. Besides, if I *had* told Ginny first, she might not have come here at all.

"Are you ready?" Mary called to me from the front door. "It's time to go."

"I'm *coming*." I pulled my jacket off its hanger with a clatter.

"Don't forget your math book," Mom reminded me.

We ran up the street to our bus stop. On the way, we saw Matt's special bus pull to the corner. At least, it's Matt's bus now. In those days he refused to ride on it. Something scared him, I guess, so Mom drove him to school herself.

Jim Briggs, another retarded child, climbed onto the bus. Jim's eight, but he's very small. Every Monday afternoon he comes to our house. His mother, a nice lady who makes good cookies, waved to us. She and Mom are good friends; they work together at the special school where Jim and Matt go.

"What's new?" Mrs. Briggs asked us cheerfully as the bus drove off.

"Mom put Matt's shirt on backwards," Mary told her, giggling.

Mrs. Briggs laughed. "Well, none of us are perfect!"

"And Matt tried to turn it around!" Mary added significantly.

"Oh!" Mrs. Briggs exclaimed, understanding at once. "Isn't that marvelous!"

It was such a relief to have someone else—someone outside the family—understand all this that I forgot about Ginny. I suddenly felt very proud of Matt. At school, before Thanksgiving, we have a long race called the Turkey Trot. Last year I came in eighth, which wasn't bad out of fifty-seven girls, but I would be very, very happy if I won. For Matt, putting his shirt on alone would be like winning the Turkey Trot.

Because of Mom's cold, Janet and I took Matt to the park after school. The park is just three blocks away. I like to walk down our street, because most of the houses have flowers in front, but you don't see many people, because the back yards are all fenced in. In Ohio, houses had two stories and no fences. It was better for playing baseball, but the weather there was always either too hot or too cold.

Everyone on our block knows Matt, but in the park it's different. That day some older children, who were swinging near the sandbox where Matt was playing, made fun of him. They laughed in a mocking way and pulled their mouths out with their fingers to make their smiles as big as his.

Mattie didn't mind. He thought they were playing with him, and he just laughed, but *I* minded. I jumped up from the bench where Janet and I were sitting, and screamed at them, "You wouldn't like it if people laughed at you for what you can't help. I hope your faces stick that way, forever and ever and ever!"

Janet didn't bother to get up. "It's no use," she said. "They'll never understand. You might as well forget it. Sit down, will you? You're just making it worse!"

I sat down again beside her and pounded my knee with my fist. "What makes people so mean?" I demanded, still watching Matt's tormentors as they started a rough game of tag.

"I don't know," Janet said. She took the rubber band off her pony tail and pulled her hair back tighter. She wrapped the rubber band back on, and then she dropped her hands loosely between her stretched-out legs. She was wearing the kind of faded jeans that have little tucks in them for decoration, and her shirttails were tied in front, over her slim tummy. "I guess people don't know what it feels like to us," she added after a pause.

"Once I found Mary and a friend of hers playing dentist with Matt," I recalled. "That was mean too."

"What did they do?"

"They poked at his teeth with a pointed thing of Mom's, the thing she cleans her fingernails with. They didn't hurt him, but still it was mean. Matt has feelings, like anybody else. He's never mean at all."

"No, he isn't," Janet agreed.

That's what makes Ginny's reaction so unfair, I was thinking when suddenly I saw Ginny herself. She was walking through the park with her mother, eating an ice-cream cone, and she pretended not to see me. I felt my face turn red.

"Isn't that your new friend?" Janet asked.

"No," I said. "I don't like her after all."

"How come?"

"Now that she's met Mattie, she acts like there's something wrong with me, too."

Janet studied her fingernail polish, first on one hand and then on the other. She chipped some of it off as she told me, "That's happened to me lots of times. It used to bother me a lot, but now it doesn't. You just have to find friends who have more to them than that."

"That's easy for *you* to say!" I retorted. "You have a best friend. So does Mary. *You* even have a boyfriend. I'm the only one who doesn't have *anyone*."

"You will," she said sympathetically. She picked up my yo-yo, which had rolled off my lap onto the ground, and handed it back to me. "Look at it like this," she said thoughtfully. "We all grew up faster because of Matt. The other kids have to catch up."

That didn't help me much. I didn't know what it felt like to be grown up. I wanted friends *now*, without waiting to grow up any more.

At least Janet understood what I was going through, and that *did* help. Janet is very special. I looked at her, sitting there beside me on the bench, and thought how pretty she was. She could do almost anything she wanted to. She could draw well, and she had a good singing voice, and she was *fun*. She was on the student council, too. We were all proud of her for that. It was nice to have this time alone with her in the park. Usually she came home late, and she always had lots of homework, and when she wasn't studying, she went out on dates, so I didn't see her as much as I would like.

Matt was having a good time, digging in the sand. He threw sand in another kid's eyes, but after Janet had stopped that by moving him somewhere else, he was fine until it was time to leave. He didn't want to leave. He bounced up and started running across the park as fast as he could. Janet and I chased after him, but we didn't catch him until he bumped into a two-year-old at the other side of the park.

"Come on, Mattie," Janet said, holding on tight to his arm.

He kicked her shin, and she let go because it hurt. I was behind him. I grabbed him around the middle, but he squirmed loose and picked up the other child's toy truck. He was mad at us, and so he smashed the truck against the ground. The other child started to cry, and his mother rushed over and took away the truck. That just made Matt angrier. He lay down on the ground and kicked his feet and flung his arms around so that we couldn't get near to pick him up.

"Oh, God," said Janet. "Why did he have to do this *now?*"

Everyone was watching us, but no one tried to help. The kids who had made fun of Matt earlier came over. They stood around and stared without making a sound. It was a nightmare for me. At least Ginny didn't see *this*.

Finally Janet got hold of his ankles and I sat on his middle. Mattie sobbed. Tears streamed all over his face, but we didn't let go until he was quiet. I tried to pretend to myself that no one else was around.

Then, quite suddenly, it was over. Mattie's body relaxed. I stood up and Janet let go of his legs. Matt bounced onto his feet and smiled as if nothing had happened. My breath poured out of me, and I realized suddenly that I had been holding it for a long time. Janet picked her bag up off the ground and slung it over her shoulder. We took Mattie's hands and marched him home as fast as we could.

Of course, Matt did catch the cold. Maybe that's why he was so awful in the park. His nose ran and ran. I felt sorry for him, because I hate to have a cold myself; for him, it's even worse. Slime dripped into his mouth in a disgusting way. Ginny would have been horrified. Even *I* couldn't look at it. He needed a really good blow.

I wiped his nose and tried to teach him. "Do this, Matt." I showed him.

He thought it was a game. He blew through his mouth.

"Through your nose, Mattie."

He pulled a handful of Kleenex out of the box and held it to *my* nose. Then he laughed.

"Now *your* nose."

Either he didn't get it or he didn't want the game to end. Sometimes it's hard to tell which. "Oh, well."

He had to stay very quiet because his heart is weak. Matt doesn't understand that, though. He just thinks that staying in the playpen goes with having a cold.

"Never mind, Matt," I told him. "When I have a cold, I have to stay home too."

Mom gets fussy when Matt is sick. She fussed at Mary for forgetting to feed her puppy, and she scolded me for losing my jacket when it wasn't really lost at all. It was in my closet the whole time; it had just fallen down so I couldn't see it under the shoes and things.

Finally Matt got well and everyone's temper improved. Matt went back to school. "At last," said Mom, "I'll have a little time."

Days later Matt hooked his fingers into his lips and pulled his mouth out of shape. His eyes crossed and he looked like a circus clown, half funny, half sad. Mary and I laughed, which delighted Matt. He did it over and over. But when Mom saw it, she said firmly, "No, don't do that, Matt!" She held his hands down at his sides. "Who showed him that?"

Then the scene in the park came rushing back to me. "Some mean kids," I said. "They copied him, and now he's copying them."

Mom sighed. I looked from her sad face to Mattie's puzzled one, and suddenly I felt all empty inside.

3

My class was going to give a party. Some of the children were doing a skit, and the rest of us were to read poems we had written. Our parents were all invited to come.

I waited to ask Mom until she was alone in the kitchen. She was busy cutting up beans for supper. Through the kitchen window she kept an eye on Matt and Peter, who were playing with a ball in the patio.

I sat down opposite her and picked up another knife. While we worked on the beans, I told her about the party. "It's Friday afternoon. *Please* won't you come. It's going to be so nice!"

Mom sighed and stopped cutting for a minute. She said slowly, "You know I can't. I can't take Matt to a thing like that."

"You never come to *anything*," I said accusingly.

"I know I don't." She sighed again.

I frowned; it sounded like the end of the conversation, and I didn't want to let Mom off until she had given me a real answer. "Couldn't Janet stay with Mattie?"

"She'll be in school."

"Or Mrs. Briggs? You baby-sit for *her*."

"She works on Fridays." She finished the last bean and got up to put water in the bowl. "Thanks for your help," she said, and then added, "If it were just Peter, it would be different."

"You tell *us* not to be ashamed of Mattie, but then *you* are," I said at her back.

Mom turned to look at me; she looked me straight in the eye. "I'm not ashamed," she said firmly. "It's no one's fault. It just is."

Just then Peter opened the door and came in for a

drink of water. Mom filled his glass at the faucet and turned to hand it to him. She didn't see Matt, who had followed Peter. He stumbled over her foot as she handed Peter the glass. Automatically, she picked Matt up in her arms and pressed him close to her. It looks funny when she lifts him like a baby because he's so big. This time it made me mad.

"You never pick *me* up like that," I said bitterly. "I never even get to sit next to you. It's always Peter and Mattie." I knew it was silly, but I said it anyway.

Mom smiled, and that made me madder. She put Matt down and pretended to try to pick me up where I still sat in my chair at the table. "What a load," she teased. "Can't seem to lift it."

I knew she was trying to change my mood by making me laugh, so I tried hard not to smile, but finally I couldn't help it. Then she said, "I'm sorry about the party. I'd like to come, but sometimes everything just gets to be too much for me. All the people in this family have so many different needs."

I remembered then that Mom wasn't going to Janet's glee club concert, either, and I felt sorry I had thought only of me.

"It's all right," I said. "Don't feel bad. I understand."

She hugged me then and said, "You know, I love each of you for yourself. You I love because you're strong and kind. But children like Mattie need so *much* love, so much tenderness. It's all they have."

I buried my face in her shoulder.

"Would you read your poem to me at home?" she asked.

"It's at school," I answered, "but I'll bring it home after the party." I felt better then, so I didn't mind when Matt grabbed a toy from Peter and Mom had to let go of me to separate them.

I went into the living room to watch TV, and Mattie followed me. A TV commercial for face cream caught Mattie's eye. He stared at the screen with great interest. Then he ran back to the kitchen. Through the doorway, I saw him plunge his hand into the butter dish.

"*What* are you doing, Matt?" Mom cried, grabbing the butter away.

Mattie had already smeared butter on his cheek. He shut his eyes, tilted his head, and rubbed his buttery face with a slow, circular motion. His mouth curled up in a blissful smile. Mom and I burst out laughing together. His imitation of that unreal TV lady was perfect.

"Janet should have seen that," I giggled. "She spends hours putting on make-up." As I washed Mattie's face, I thought to myself that *I* might be silly sometimes, but never as silly as *that*!

The day of the school party, though, my hurt feeling came back. Everyone's mother was there but mine! I felt small and alone. Ginny's mother looked beautiful. She was wearing a blue suit with a red-and-white silk scarf at her neck. She was tall and slim and elegant. Ginny held her hand proudly all the time.

The other children served punch and cookies to their mothers. I stood in line with everyone else, but I gave my glass of punch to my teacher since Mom wasn't there. "Thank you, Sarah," Miss Williams said. "That was thoughtful of you." I would have stayed with her, but she had to go around the room and talk to all the mothers.

The noise in the room gave me a headache. There were too many people. I kept moving around so that none of my friends would notice I was alone. I looked at the artwork on the walls, although it had been hanging there for at least a week. I thought my own picture was the best, and I wished Mom had seen it on the wall. She would like it when I brought it home, but she wouldn't know it was the best in my class.

At last Miss Williams asked everyone to sit down and be quiet. We sang a song, and then the skit began. We children sat on the floor in front, and the grownups sat on chairs behind. I hardly watched because I was going over my poem in my mind.

After the skit came the poems. Ginny's turn came before mine. Her poem was about her pet turtle. After she had read it, she went back and stood by her mother's chair. Her mother clapped loudly, with her hands way out in front of her.

My poem was about friends. It rhymed and had four lines. I was so nervous beforehand that I had crumpled the paper all up without noticing. My poem went like this:

Friends are people who really care.
When you need them, they're always there.
With friends, it's easy to share,
So you can be happy anywhere.

I really meant my poem to be for Ginny, but I don't think she was listening. She was too excited, and she whispered into her mother's ear as I read my lines.

Afterward I quickly sat down again on the floor. I was blushing and didn't look at anyone. I heard the audience clap, but I knew it wasn't *special* clapping, because I wasn't their child.

Mom came to pick me up at school. I saw her car in the parking lot when the bell rang and I went out to catch the bus. I would have asked her to come in and see my picture, but she had Peter and Mattie with her. I thought if she had really wanted to, she would have managed somehow to come earlier, in time for the party. So I just climbed in the front and slammed the car door without saying anything.

"How was the party?" Mom asked, but when I merely shrugged she didn't press it. "I had to go for groceries," she explained, "so I thought I'd save you a ride on the bus. Mary's playing soccer, so she'll be late getting home."

At the store she bought me a comic book. She had never done that before, because she didn't really approve of them. I love comic books, but that day I didn't want it. I didn't thank her, because it seemed like a bribe and it didn't make up for her not coming to the party. "What do you say?" she asked crossly. I said, "Thanks," but in a very low voice so she would know I didn't completely mean it.

Mom put Matt in the shopping cart and carried Peter on her hip. I pushed the cart along while she looked for things on her list.

Matt kept reaching for everything. His arms are short, but they're long when he wants something. He knocked a box of cereal off the shelf, and then a can of soup. He almost got a jar of mayonnaise, but I moved the cart just in time. "Keep it in the center of the aisle," Mom said impatiently.

Then I discovered that if I jiggled the cart, Mattie forgot about reaching for things. He laughed and laughed. I love to make Mattie laugh. He laughs the way no one else laughs, all the way through him. I jiggled the cart, and his head bounced, and he laughed like that. He reached out and touched my face, which meant, "More, more."

I began to run down the aisle, pushing the cart as

fast as I could. I heard Mom scream, "Sarah!" in a high, scared voice. Then the cart crashed into another cart that I hadn't seen. People turned around and glared at me, and Mom exploded.

She shook my arm and tried to make me look at her. "I've just about had it with you today," she said so that all the store could hear. "One more trick like that, and I'll spank! You've been pushing me to the limit. If you don't think I'd dare spank you in public, just try one more thing!"

Mattie pulled himself up in the cart and waved his arms in glee at this lecture. Peter thought it was funny, too, and jiggled the cart a little himself to see what Mom would do, but she ignored him and held the cart steady with one hand on the rim and a foot against one wheel. She went on scolding me; then her anger seemed to give out. "Use your head a little," she said when she was calmer. "He might have fallen out." She was still upset, but she never did actually punish me. I think she knew I still felt unhappy about the party.

The next day I found myself standing next to Ginny while we waited for the library to open before school. We were both embarrassed because we hadn't really spoken to each other since Ginny had come to my house.

"How come your mother didn't come to the party?" she asked me. Her voice sounded stiff, and she twitched her head in an awkward way.

"Peter was sick," I lied. I tried hard not to let my face show the dismay I felt on learning that she *had* noticed after all.

"Oh," Ginny said after a pause. "That's too bad." Her voice sounded softer. "I thought probably she didn't want to bring your *other* brother."

My face turned hot. I looked down and didn't answer. 2082445

"My mother says children like that shouldn't live at home," she added. "It isn't fair to the others."

Now I realize she meant to be sympathetic, trying in a clumsy way to put herself in my place. This was the first time she had even mentioned Matt at all. Maybe she wanted to talk about him or explain how she had felt, but I didn't understand that then. She didn't say it the right way. She just made me feel worse. It was one thing for *me* to resent Matt; I had to live with him. But for Ginny to pity me was *not* all right.

"Where would they go, then?" I asked indignantly.

Ginny tilted her head to one side and looked at me out of half-closed eyes. Her mouth puckered. "I'm not sure," she admitted. "I guess there are special places."

I was too shocked to reply. It had never occurred to me that Matt might live somewhere else.

4

By now Ginny had made other friends. She spent a lot of time with Betty Evans and Laura Sprankle, two of the most popular girls at school. Laura had won a medal for gymnastics. I admired the way she walked and wished that I was graceful like her. Betty, her close friend, was rather the opposite. Betty was pudgy but so good-natured that everyone liked her.

I would have liked to play with Laura and Betty, but they had never really noticed me. It hurt me that

Ginny, who had just come, was so quickly accepted into their group, while I, after two years, had never been included. Ginny and Laura and Betty whispered together every day at recess. I felt very left out.

Several times I asked Ginny if she could play after school, but she always said no. I even offered to share some money I had earned watching Matt and Peter if she would go with me to the drugstore. She hesitated then. I was sure she wanted to accept, but in the end she said she couldn't do it that day.

"Don't you like me any more?" I asked her.

"It isn't that," she said uncomfortably.

"What, then?"

"Nothing," she insisted. "I can't play, that's all."

One day, just as school let out, I noticed that Ginny had left a notebook out on her desk. I thought I would do her a favor by putting it away—until I saw that it said, "Secret, Keep Out!" across the top.

I glanced around. Most of the children had already left the room, and the teacher was putting on her coat. Her back was turned. I wavered. Then, very quickly, I slipped Ginny's notebook into my book bag.

I knew it was wrong—I didn't like what I did—but

I simply *had* to know what she had written and whether it was about me. I would bring it back early the next day before she had a chance to miss it.

At home I went straight to my room and shut the door. I sat on the edge of my bed and took the notebook out of my bag. My hands were shaking, and I felt as if someone were watching over my shoulder. Trembling, I read the minutes of a secret club. Ginny Foster was president, Laura Sprankle vice-president, Betty Evans secretary. So *that* was what they always whispered about. I didn't read further. I already knew enough.

Mary, who shared my room, would be home from school soon. I shut the notebook and put it under another book on my desk so she wouldn't see it. My desk was very neat because Mom had made me clean it up just the day before. That's why I had to hide the notebook under something. I guess I didn't want to see it myself, either, and be reminded of what I had done.

"Would you mind watching the boys for half an hour?" Mom called down the hall. "I need to run down to the store. I won't be long."

"Do I *have* to?" I complained. I needed to be alone for a while.

"Please do it for me," Mom begged. "It's *so* much easier if I can go alone." Her tone of voice reminded me of our last trip to the store.

"Oh, all right." I gave in reluctantly. "Hurry back, though."

I turned on the television in the living room and sank into the sofa. Peter was building with blocks, and Matt was watching from the playpen. He reached through the net for a block, but it was too far away. He wailed with frustration.

"Be quiet, Mattie. I can't hear my show."

I gave him a rubber duck, and he was happy for a while, squeaking the duck. Then Peter came too close to the pen. Matt's arm shot out again. He grabbed Peter's hair. Now Peter yelled. I pried Matt's fingers open and gave Matt and Peter graham crackers to keep them quiet, but Mattie dropped his crackers out of the pen and cried again, so I sat him down on the couch beside me.

Peter, meanwhile, had lost interest in his blocks. He pushed open the sliding glass doors and went out to the patio. That was all right, because the gate was closed.

The TV movie was exciting and took my mind off Ginny's club, but I couldn't watch it for long. A bee stung Peter, and I had to rush outside. The bee was still there inside his hand.

I couldn't find any baking soda in our cupboard, so I ran next door to borrow some. When I came back, I put the soda on Peter's hand, washed his face, and cuddled him until he stopped crying.

Suddenly I remembered Matt. He wasn't in the living room any more. I searched the house. The last place I looked was my own room, at the end of the hall. There sat Matt in the middle of the floor. Around him were books and papers and all sorts of stuff. My heart sank. Joyfully he shredded a piece of paper and chewed the pieces. He smiled up at me for my approval.

"Oh, Mattie!"

For the first instant I was too shocked to be angry. Then I saw Ginny's notebook. It lay open with half the pages ripped out. The notes about the secret club were scattered all around.

"You're a bad, bad boy!" I screamed, rushing into the room. *"Bad, bad!"* At that moment I hated Mattie for all the trouble he caused. I forgot I was the one who had brought the notebook home. I just blamed Mattie for the mess I was in now.

Mattie didn't move. I jerked him up off the floor by his collar and spanked him as hard as I could. His diapers protected him, so I mostly hurt my own hand. His face puckered up as he tried to understand, but he didn't cry.

Then I lost my head. I picked up a shoe and whammed him with it. I don't know how many times I hit him. It seemed as if someone else were doing it, not me. I didn't hear Mom come into the house or down the hall, either. Suddenly she was just there. She grabbed me by the shoulders and spun me around. Her eyes bulged with anger, and at first she was too mad to speak. "What am I going to do with you?" she said at last in a high, frenzied voice. "You go from bad to worse. Where does all this hatred come from? I should have spanked you in the store. Maybe that would have ended it all."

She let go of me roughly. Then she knelt down and gathered Mattie up in her arms. She kissed his wet cheeks over and over and rocked his trembling body back and forth, back and forth. He clung to her and sobbed. Finally he was still, as if he had gone to sleep.

Only then did Mom turn back to me. I was trembling as much as Matt had, but she didn't comfort me. Her face was dead white. She seemed very far away from me. "Sarah," she said in a strange, overcalm voice, "you will stay in your room for the rest of the afternoon. And you will not be allowed to go to the movies with Ginny on Saturday. I hope that will get the point across."

"Ginny invited me?" I stammered, everything else swept out of my mind.

She nodded. "I saw her and her mother at the store."

"Oh, *please—please* let me!"

"I can't allow violence," she said in a warmer voice.

"But look at what *Mattie* did."

"I know, I know." She shook her head sadly. "Even so, you can't give in to your feelings that way. I have to make you realize the harm you might have done."

She took Mattie out, and I closed the door. I flopped across my bed and sobbed and sobbed. Mary came in a while later and asked what was wrong, but I didn't respond, so she left again.

At dinner hardly anyone spoke. My eyes stung from

crying, and my nose ran. "What's the matter with Sarah?" Dad asked.

"She's being punished," Mom replied. She went on feeding Matt without saying anything more.

I watched Mattie suck applesauce off his spoon, half of it running down his chin, and I looked away. I felt sick and angry. "It was Matt's fault," I said bitterly. "He wrecked my room. It's his fault I don't have any friends. Nobody wants to come here because of him. Now, because of him—because of what he did—I can't go to Ginny's either. Matt should live somewhere else. It isn't fair to us."

"Who told you that?" Dad demanded sternly.

I stared at my plate. "It's obvious."

Dad said carefully, "There's no easy solution. I don't think you understand, Sarah, how tough the choices are."

"You don't understand how hard it is for *me*," I said, and neither Dad nor Mom replied.

Mary helped me pick up our room. She didn't say a word about *her* things being messed up. I was very grateful for that. After a while I told her what had happened.

"I had borrowed this notebook from Ginny," I began, "and Matt tore it up. That's what really got to me. Now I can't return it. Ginny's going to be just furious. Now we'll *never* be friends."

"Buy her another," Mary suggested. She sat backwards on her desk chair, with her hands on the back and her chin resting on her hands, and looked at me thoughtfully.

"I can't," I moaned. "She had written in it. That's the whole trouble." I was sitting dejectedly on the edge of the lower bunk. My foot played with a slipper on the floor until it slid away from me under the bed.

"You shouldn't have left it out," Mary said. "You know nothing's safe around here."

"I didn't. That is, it was on my desk. *What* am I going to tell Ginny?"

"Just tell her the truth," Mary said. "What else?"

"I don't know." I sighed. "I wish it were so simple." I couldn't quite admit my own role in this trouble. Mary would never have taken the book in the first place. She would be shocked if I told her. I came back to Matt. "I didn't mean to hurt him—I *didn't* hurt him that much. Do you think I was awful?"

"No," Mary said slowly. She turned around on her chair so that I couldn't see her face, and she got out her homework. "He needs to know when he's bad, same as us. If only you hadn't used a shoe . . ."

"I know. That was a mistake," I said hastily. What I had done seemed a little less terrible, put that way.

"Yes."

Suddenly I heard Dad's measured footsteps in the hall. For an instant I froze. Then I silently slipped off my bed and turned the lock on the door. Mary pretended to study her book.

Dad knocked gently. "May I come in?" he asked. My heart pounded, but I didn't answer. I waited without moving so much as a finger. He tried the knob, and then he said, "Sarah, perhaps it would help if we had a little talk."

"No!" I said loudly. "I know what you're going to say, and it wouldn't help."

He waited a little. "Are you sure?"

"Yes," I replied in a voice that sounded far from sure, even to me.

There was a long pause before he said, "All right," and I heard his footsteps retreating down the hall.

46

Later that night, when we were trying to sleep, Mary and I heard tense voices rising and falling, pushing and straining against each other.

"They must be arguing about you," Mary said from the bed above me.

"Or Mattie," I replied. My voice sounded tiny and rough in the dark, like the croak of a tree frog. Once more I felt sick, as if my insides were falling, falling away, dragging the rest of my body after them. For hours I couldn't sleep.

Finally I heard Mary's breathing deepen. Then I was really alone with my thoughts. What had made me behave as I had? I wondered. I didn't like myself for taking Ginny's book, and I didn't like myself for taking my feelings out on poor Mattie, but I had done these things. What did it mean? Why had I somehow mixed Mattie up with Ginny and myself?

At last it came to me quite calmly that *I* needed to change. Maybe there was something in me that other kids didn't trust. Maybe I got upset too easily and then blamed other people for things I had done. In a way I was glad to be punished this time. It even occurred to me that Mom might have been right; if she *had* spanked me in the supermarket, I might not have done something worse.

I felt lighter when I figured this out. Then I thought again of Mattie—might they really send him away? Dad hadn't said, "We would never dream of that!" He had said instead, "There's no easy solution," and there had been uncertainty in his voice.

Sure, I had wished this afternoon that Mattie would disappear. I wished *I* could disappear too! But I only *said* Matt should live somewhere else to test what Mom and Dad would say. I didn't really mean it; at least, I didn't mean it now that I had worked it all through. Now, with all my soul, I hoped that nothing would ever happen to hurt Mattie again.

~5

In the morning my eyes were red and swollen. I felt tired and puffy all over. I drenched my face in cold water, but it only helped a little.

Dad was leaving on one of his trips. I passed him in the hall as he was taking his suitcase out to the car. He put his hand on my forehead and tipped it back to look into my face. "You help your mother," he said, meaning much more than that. "I'll see you in a couple of days."

I wriggled loose. I was *glad* he was going away. He looked too deeply into me.

Ginny was late for school. She slid into her seat just after the bell rang. Her mother must have driven her. There was no chance to speak to her until recess.

"Thanks for inviting me to the movies," I said hesitantly. "I'd really like to go, but I'm being punished."

"What did you do?"

"I hit Matt," I said, and felt better for saying it openly to someone.

"Oh," Ginny said. Her eyes seemed to pull back the way they did when Matt was there. "Did you hurt him?"

"No."

For an instant our eyes met. Ginny smiled a little. Then she looked away. She rubbed the back of her leg with her other foot. Neither of us spoke. I wanted to tell her about the notebook, but my tongue plugged up my throat like a dry, tight cork. I couldn't seem to say anything at all.

The chance went by. Betty Evans asked Ginny to play, and she skipped away. With a kind of relief I swung on the bars, back and forth from one end to the other, until my arms felt like rubber bands, with no power of their own.

Matt was very quiet that day. When I got home, he smiled at me and gurgled a happy sound. I knelt down and hugged him around the middle. He nuzzled his face into my shoulder.

"Have you forgiven me, Mattie?" I asked, but Matt just laughed. His hand found my hair ribbon, and his stubby fingers fumbled to undo the bow. Grinning, he trailed the ribbon across his own hair. For a moment it dangled over his nose. His eyes crossed, trying to pin the ribbon between them. His tongue went out to taste it.

"What a clown you are, Mattie!"

Who else forgives so easily? I thought. He laughed and waved the ribbon in my face, trying in his clumsy way to tickle my nose.

The social worker came that afternoon. I didn't know she was coming until I saw her blue car drive up. "Mom," I called out, "Mrs. Manley's here!"

I wondered if Mom had asked her to come because of what I had done yesterday, but Mom groaned and said, "Why is it I'm never ready? Hang up that jacket, Sarah, and *whose* dirty socks are those under the couch?" While Mrs. Manley walked stiffly up the walk, Mom flew around, straightening magazines and whisking toys into a box.

Peter had gotten into the pots and pans, and there were lids all over the kitchen floor. Mattie was in there too, banging lids together. They both loved this game. Just as the bell rang, Mom and I heard a loud crash. Then Matt cried.

"You go to the door, Sarah. I'll be there in a minute."

I opened the door for Mrs. Manley and asked her to sit down. Mrs. Manley has long, straight blond hair and wears gold-rimmed Granny glasses. She doesn't look much older than Janet. That day she had on a long, full purple dress with little flowers all over it, and sandals. She always tries to be very friendly, but she can never think of anything better to say to me than, "What did you do at school today?" Then she gets down to business. She puts a very serious expression on her face and begins asking questions. While I'm trying to think of an answer, she doodles in her notebook. Then she writes furiously to get every word down.

Today she asked me if I loved my little brother. I knew she meant Matt, because Matt is the reason for her coming every month, but I asked, "Which one?"

She blushed then and said, "Well, I meant Matt especially."

"He's not as little as Peter," I pointed out. "They act about the same. Sometimes they're okay and sometimes they're not."

"How do you feel about Matt *today*?" she insisted.

I squirmed. "Well, better than yesterday," I said finally.

"And how did you feel yesterday?"

"I was mad."

"Just mad?"

I nodded.

"Why were you mad?"

"I don't really want to talk about it," I said.

From the kitchen Mattie's sobs sounded like a fish gasping for air. Mrs. Manley's eyes rolled in that direction. I took advantage of her pause to escape. I jumped up from the couch and ran to see what had happened.

Mom was washing blood off Matt's face.

"He must have tripped over a lid and hit his head. The cupboard door was open. Get me a Band-aid, will you? It's only a scratch, but it looks awful."

Mrs. Manley followed me down the hall to the bathroom. "What happened, what happened?" she asked nervously. She always says everything twice.

"Matt fell."

The bathroom was a mess. Mrs. Manley wasn't supposed to come down there. There were diapers in the sink, and Janet's hair curlers and face goo and nail scissors were spread all over the counter. Someone had left a towel on the floor. While I reached for the Band-aids, I shoved it toward the corner with my feet. That way it looked like part of the laundry pile.

Mrs. Manley followed me back to the kitchen. While Mom put a Band-aid on Matt's forehead, I picked up pots and pans. "Can I help, can I help?" asked Mrs. Manley, hovering over Mom and Mattie.

"He's all right now," Mom said.

"You can help *me*," I suggested. Mrs. Manley looked very much surprised. She picked up one pot and then she went back into the living room to wait for Mom.

I retreated to my room and tried to listen from there. What would Mom say about yesterday? After a while I heard Mom's voice getting louder and more excited. She always tells us to be superpolite to Mrs. Manley, but now she was arguing with her. I couldn't help feeling pleased.

After Mrs. Manley left, the house was very quiet. I found Mom sitting on the couch with her face buried in her hands.

"What's the matter?"

She didn't answer at once, and that alarmed me more. "I'm afraid I was rude," she said finally.

"What did you say?"

"I told her she didn't know anything about kids!"

I giggled. "That's *true*! It's not rude to say something that's true."

"She's never changed a diaper in her life," Mom went on, "but she sure has all the answers! Her head's stuffed full of textbook nonsense." Her eyes flashed.

"I'm *glad* you told her that," I said with glee.

Mom sat back and laughed. "Well, I didn't quite say *all* that!"

"Did you see her face when I asked her to help?"

I asked with great amusement. I was enjoying this conversation now.

Mom nodded and wiped the corners of her eyes. She was still unhappy, though, in spite of laughing.

"What did she say about *me*?" I asked cautiously after a moment.

"Not much." She paused. "We talked mostly about Matt."

I laughed with relief. I knew Mom had told Mrs. Manley on the phone what had happened yesterday—otherwise, she wouldn't have come today—but at least they hadn't discussed it with me around. Still, on reflection, I knew they must have said *something*.

"What did she say about Matt?" I probed.

"Oh, I don't know." Mom sighed. "She feels he's not progressing as he should." Her tone was evasive.

"What does that mean?"

"She said he should have more speech lessons. He gets that at school—or I thought he did. And she said we don't work with him enough on balance. He should sit on that T-stool twenty times a day."

The T-stool is just a board nailed to the end of a short, round leg. "I can't even sit on that," I protested, picking it up off the floor and trying to balance it on the soft cushion of the couch.

"Well, I brought it out," Mom said, "and Matt did what he always does. He picked it up and banged the floor with it. He doesn't like that stool. He's afraid he'll fall off."

"He's right. He would."

"Then I took him on my lap, and she told me I shouldn't reward him when he doesn't do what I want!" She turned her hands out in a gesture of help-lessness.

Very vividly I pictured Mom holding Mattie on her lap. I saw them, not here in the living room with Mrs. Manley, but on the floor of my room. "Mattie *needed* to be held after hurting himself," I said. "How dare she say things like that?"

Mom didn't answer me. "She's not even consistent," she went on. "First she calls the environment hostile, then she says I overcompensate! Personally, I think *her* solution stinks!"

"What is her solution?" I asked timidly.

"Not to deal with life at all!" Mom replied, slapping her knee. She set her chin defiantly and stared straight ahead. Her eyes seemed to burn a hole through the wooden paneling of the wall. I looked where she was looking, but there was nothing there, not even a picture, just the yellow-brown plywood wall, with scratches where someone bumped it, I guess.

Somehow I knew Mom had just told me the important thing. Mrs. Manley *had* said something that would affect us all. I didn't understand, yet I didn't dare to ask. Mom was telling me without telling me. I wanted to know, yet I didn't.

I poked at a hole in the upholstery of the couch without thinking. Mom moved my hand away from the hole. Then her body sagged against a cushion. "I do the best I can," she said. "I've tried to work with the stool, but I can't force him."

"No."

"We can't afford more special lessons. Mary wants ballet lessons, and we can't afford that either. Who's to say which is more important? Besides, at the county school, they tell me just the opposite. *They* say Matt's doing all we can expect."

The danger, whatever it was, had passed. I moved closer to Mom. "*I* think he's making progress," I said to comfort her. "Think of the shirt and how he knew it was on backwards."

Mom nodded, but she was crying now. I had hardly ever seen her cry. I put my arm around her shoulders. I didn't know what to say.

"She makes me feel I should be doing something more. Am I really holding him back?"

"No!" I insisted. "She has no right to come here and make you cry when Dad isn't even here."

"That's part of the problem." Mom sighed, wiping her eyes. "He's away so much. I have to handle so much alone."

"Next time I won't let her in!" I said indignantly.

"No, no," Mom said quietly. "That's no solution. She tries to be helpful, and maybe she's right. I'm going to take an evening course in child development. Maybe that will help. Besides, she had one other good suggestion. Do you know what that was?"

"What?"

"A birthday party."

"For Mattie?"

"For *you*, silly! It's your birthday that comes soon."

"Oh!" I exclaimed, but then I wasn't sure. I thought

of Ginny and wondered whether she would come.

"What's the matter?" Mom asked after a moment.

"Nothing."

"You're frowning."

"I was just wondering. . ." I began, and then stopped.

"What were you wondering?"

"Would Mattie have to be there?" I asked, ashamed.

"I see," Mom said. "No, I'm sure we can work something out."

~6

Afterward I wondered a lot about what Mrs. Manley could have said to upset Mom so much, but I couldn't figure it out. Besides, I had my birthday party to think about now.

I sat down right away to make my birthday list. No one had had a party since Matt was born, so I felt very special. I wrote down twelve names, starting with Ginny's, and I looked up all the phone numbers. "Can I start inviting people?"

"Just a *minute*," Mom said. "We have to plan."

"I already have. We can decorate the patio with balloons and things and barbecue hamburgers. Okay?"

"Well, I guess. It's Friday, so there's no school the next day."

"Why don't you go to Great America?" Mary said. "Susan took me there last year. It was the greatest."

"How many kids did she have?"

"Three."

"That's the trouble. It costs too much. I want a *real* party, with lots of people."

"You just want lots of presents."

"I do not!"

"I don't see why it's you who gets the party," she mumbled so Mom wouldn't hear, "after what you did."

I glared at her. "My birthday comes first."

"Girls, girls," Mom said.

"I wish *I* could have a dance," Mary said. "Not a birthday party—an evening party not on my birthday, like the ones Janet goes to."

Dad came in, carrying his suitcase, just in time to hear that last sentence. "Aren't you a bit young for that?" he said.

"I'll be thirteen soon!"

Dad laughed. That upset Mary. She frowned and left the room, while the rest of us gathered around Dad to hear about his trip.

I felt sorry for Mary. After all, she was right—she deserved a party more than I did. I thought about it for three days, and then I said to her, "If you want, it could be a party for both of us. We could both invite friends and not have the presents. Only I don't really want boys—okay?"

"Thanks," Mary said, "but it's all right. This is your birthday. I'll wait till I can have my own party some other time."

Janet said that since it was October we should have Halloween decorations.

"Would you help?"

"I guess. Maybe Steve would take us to get pumpkins." Steve is Janet's boyfriend, and he has a driver's license.

"Oh, that would be nice!"

"I'll make the cake," Janet offered. "What kind do you want?"

"Chocolate, with white icing."

"Okay."

I felt like hugging Janet for being so nice.

Steve was nice, too. He borrowed his Dad's pickup truck and drove us all the way down to Morgan Hill, where there are lots of farm stands. We could have gotten a pumpkin right in San Jose, but Steve likes to drive. Janet rode in the front and sat close to Steve. Mary and I sat in the back and spied on them. We made funny faces at truck drivers, too, although we're really too big for that.

We bought lots of little pumpkins, and we carved jack-o'-lanterns with all kinds of faces. Matt was very excited. He wanted to carve one too. "Knives are sharp, Matt," I told him. "Knives can hurt." I put his finger on the edge of the blade to show him, but he jerked his hand back and tried again to take my knife away. Finally Janet put him in the house. He was very frustrated and stood with his hands on the glass doors, looking out with his saddest face. All afternoon he made an awful noise, like a pig oinking. Nobody could persuade him to stop. It was funny at first, but after a while it drove us all crazy.

We put the pumpkins up high along the fence so

that the boys couldn't reach them. We strung crepe-paper streamers from the roof to the apricot tree in the corner of the yard. Janet drew a wonderful witch on a big piece of black paper, and I cut it out and nailed it to the fence.

Everybody I invited was coming to the party except one girl. When I asked Ginny, I almost said, "Matt won't be there," but then I didn't. If she didn't like me well enough to come anyway, then I didn't want her. At first Ginny said she'd have to ask her mother, who was out. That made me nervous, but later she called back and said she could come.

The day of the party I rushed home from school and changed into my best dress. "Wait a little," Mom pleaded. "The party doesn't start till five. You don't want to get dirty yet."

"I *won't.*"

Together, we spread a cloth over the picnic table and set out cups and forks and paper plates. Then I went around the yard and hid clues for the treasure hunt that Mary and I had made up. I let Mattie help me hide them, since he was missing the party. He stuck one between the boards of the back fence. We put the last clue in a crack in a half-dead branch of the apricot tree. It said to go inside for the treasure. The treasure was a leather-bound diary that locks!

It was almost time for the party to begin. "Now I'll drive the boys over to the sitter's, and I'll be right back," Mom said. "Where did Matt go? I thought he was in the patio with you."

We both noticed at once that the gate was open. Mom groaned. "Stay here with Peter while I look for him. He can't have gone very far."

Janet was putting the finishing touches on the cake. "Here, Peter. You can lick the bowl."

"That's lovely!" I cried. "How did you make those pumpkins? Oh, I *love* the cat!"

"I made a cone out of paper and squeezed the icing through it," Janet said. She was pleased herself.

Mom came back now. "I can't find him," she said in a scared voice. "You'll have to help look."

"But the party—it's almost time."

"First things first."

"I'll help," Mary offered. She and I ran up and down the street calling Matt. No answer: he didn't appear.

Tears of anger gushed up in my eyes. "He's going to

spoil everything! Why does this always happen to me?"

"Maybe he went to visit Jim."

We knocked at Jim's house, but no one was home. We knocked at some other houses too, but no one had seen him.

"How 'bout the park?" Mary suggested. "He knows his way there."

We raced each other the whole three blocks. He wasn't in the sandbox or around the jungle gyms or swings. "The john," Mary said. "That's the only other place."

We looked in both sides. I stood outside to guard while Mary checked the men's side, but Matt wasn't there.

"Maybe they've found him by now."

We walked home quickly. I knew I was going to be late for my own party, and I felt awful. From a block away I could see two cars parked in front of our house. Girls were getting out, carrying packages, but how could we even *have* a party now?

Mom was on the telephone. "*Please* come home," she was saying. "Matt's wandered off and we can't find him. Sarah's friends are here already. You've got to help with this."

There was an edge in her voice. I knew she was talking to Dad. Ever since Mrs. Manley's last visit they had been arguing about Matt. Mom wanted Dad to spend more time with him, but Dad said he couldn't leave work any earlier.

The doorbell rang again, and more girls arrived. I wanted to be gay and cheerful, but I just couldn't be. For me, the party was already spoiled. We couldn't play any games while Matt was lost. We couldn't do anything. The mood wasn't right any more. And besides that, when we *did* find him, he would be there at the party in spite of Mom's promise. Everyone would see him.

Ginny's car drove up. She walked up the path swinging her present. I smiled as I opened the door for her, but she knew right away that something was wrong. The other girls stood around not saying anything. They didn't even know where to put their presents down.

Janet ushered us all out to the patio. She tried to start some games for us, but no one seemed interested. I could hear Mom on the phone again. Then the garage door creaked. Dad was home. He came through the sliding glass doors to the patio, still carrying his brief-case. "Where's your mother?" he asked briskly.

"She's out looking again," Janet said. "She called the police already."

"Now listen, girls," Dad said in his organizing voice. "We can't start the party quite yet. Sarah's brother's missing, and we need you to help look. This is a serious situation. He's a handicapped child, and anything might happen to him. He's probably somewhere near. I want you to pick partners and each pair of girls check out two yards on this block. After that, come back here."

My friends looked at each other nervously. They weren't sure how to react or what Dad thought might happen. No one moved.

"Get going," Dad yelled. "Use imagination. This is a hunt. There'll be a prize."

"But we only have *one* prize," I told him, "and that's for the treasure hunt. I spent *hours* setting it up."

"Don't argue," Dad said. "Start looking."

Everyone moved at once then. I looked at Ginny and Ginny looked at me. "Come on." I shrugged.

We walked along the sidewalk. "I'm sorry. He was

supposed to be at the sitter's," I told her.

"It's all right," Ginny said, but she walked very slowly, as if she didn't want to have anything to do with finding Mattie.

After a while everyone drifted back. "What should we do now?" they asked.

"Just stay here," Dad said. The girls looked disappointed not to be given a new assignment, but Dad was too busy to notice.

Everyone was excited now, because a fire truck had just arrived and two policemen were talking to Mom. Neighbors were out looking, too.

Everyone but me had forgotten all about the party. By now we should have been cooking hamburgers, but we weren't. I had planned it all in my mind, but nothing I had planned was happening that way. The patio was deserted now, except for Peter, who was trying to reach a balloon. The crepe-paper streamers had already sagged a little. The candles inside the jack-o'-lanterns were burning down.

I went out front, where all the excitement was. Mom was rushing around frantically, while the girls followed the firemen and tried to think of places they hadn't already looked. Even Ginny was caught up in the hunt by this time. She thought of several new places to look, such as the garage and the little utilities room. She knew our house, because she'd been here before.

No one was paying any attention to Peter. He toddled over to the back fence and put his ear against a crack. He mumbled to himself.

"What are you saying, Peter?" I asked when I finally noticed him. "Talk right. Don't talk Mattie-talk."

"Mattie's back here," he said, clearly this time.

I listened through the crack, but I couldn't hear anything. "He can't be," I said. "He can't have gone all the way around the block. He's never been there."

"We'll go see," some of the girls offered. They raced off. They all wanted to be first to see if Peter was right.

Suddenly Mary remembered the loose board behind an oleander bush. "You don't suppose he could have squeezed through?" she said, disappearing into the thick leaves. "Hey! The board's gone!"

I was right on her heels.

"He's here!" she yelled, but the other girls had already beaten her to Matt. They ran in from the street, laughing and shoving each other to be first. "We found him!"

"No, Peter did."

Mattie sat peacefully in the middle of a vegetable garden. He had found a yellow squash and was happily poking holes into it with a stick. "Mattie, what are you doing?"

The girls stood in a circle and watched him with curiosity. They were quiet now.

"He's making a jack-o'-lantern!" Mary said. "It's obvious."

I hugged him with relief. "That's nice, that's a good jack-o'-lantern, but you scared us, Mattie," I told him, pulling him to his feet. "Now we're going home."

Ginny stood a little way back. I saw her when I turned to help Matt through the hole.

"A jack-o'-lantern," she repeated. "He was making a jack-o'-lantern."

"Yes."

She had a surprised look on her face—a thoughtful look. The fear was gone. The jack-o'-lantern must have made Matt seem human after all.

Mom laughed and cried at once when she saw Matt. She was a complete wreck from worrying so much. She took him on her lap and rocked him, but Matt didn't need that. He was excited by the fire truck and all the people.

The firemen and policemen left. Steve had come to take Janet out, but they both stayed to help with my party. Janet heated up the mulled cider and Steve lit the charcoal in the barbecue pit and put on a record.

Dad clapped his hands for quiet. "I want to thank every last one of you," he said. "We would never have found Matt without your help. You girls were terrific. Just terrific! I'd hire you as detectives any time!"

They all thought he was terrific, too. They flocked around him, all chattering at once, but Dad wasn't through. He raised his hands and said, "I'm delighted my daughter has such an outstanding group of friends. I wish I could give each and every one of you a prize to express my gratitude and appreciation."

"He sounds like he's running for President," Mary whispered to me. We both giggled.

"I do have here the prize I promised for the winner of the hunt," Dad went on ceremoniously. "Congratulations to you, Peter. You're an outstanding boy." He shook Peter's hand vigorously and presented him with a big candy bar.

"He buys those for his own lunches," Mary informed me. "Swiss chocolate, too! Boy, we never get anything like that!"

I laughed. "I *wondered* what he would find for a prize." I didn't think it was a very good one, but Peter was happy. He tore the paper off right away. "Let's give him a big hand," Dad said, and everyone clapped loudly, even Mattie.

Mattie and Peter were both part of the party now. There was no point in taking them to the sitter's. Mattie loved everything. He followed Dad around, and "helped" with the hamburgers. He danced to the music, turning in a circle, with his arms stuck up over his head, until he fell in a heap. Mattie loves music. Then he went around hugging everyone and showing off. He was so pleased that all this fuss had been made over him.

Some of the things he did were not so cute. He made his oinking noise again, and he ate food off other people's plates. If he had behaved this way when my guests first came, it would have been awful. Even now I watched anxiously to see their reaction, but no one seemed to mind. My friends hugged Mattie back, and they fed him potato chips and laughed at the funny faces he made. They were all on his side because they helped find him.

Several times he headed back toward the hole in the fence, but each time someone diverted him. It was easy to get his attention, because he thought the party, like the fire truck, was all for him.

Sometime after we had eaten the cake and I had opened my presents, Betty Evans said suddenly, "I have a cousin who's handicapped."

Other people stopped talking. "What's that?" someone asked.

"Well," she explained, "it means he's retarded, but we don't say that usually. He's handicapped because everything's harder for him."

"It can mean other things, too, can't it?" Laura asked.

"Sure," Dad told her. "You're handicapped if you can't walk, or if you're blind, or if you have only one arm."

"That's what I thought." Laura nodded.

The patio was quiet for a minute. "How *old* is Mattie?" one girl asked then, and someone else asked, "Why does he look like that?" Then everyone began asking questions about Matt and handicapped kids. They must have been holding these questions inside them ever since they came. They weren't mean questions, just *questions*. It was all right. I felt proud to know about something most of the girls never even heard of. Most of them had never heard of Down's syndrome, which is another name for what Mattie has. Some of them never even knew that kids like Matt went to school. "Sure they do," I said. "They learn how to keep their balance and talk better and how to take care of themselves." They could all see this was important, since Mattie had just been lost. As we talked about it, some kind of knot let go inside me, and a loose, happy feeling—a birthday feeling—came in.

~7

After my birthday party, Ginny was different. All the stiffness had gone out of her manner. Finally I got up my courage to tell her about the notebook. She surprised me by replying, "I knew you had it."

"How?"

"Just the way you behaved. You acted guilty all the time."

"Did I? Well, I felt bad. I'd never do it again."

She already knew that, though. She pushed back her

hair and smiled in a serious kind of way. "Could I come over to your house after school?" she asked.

"Of course!" I exclaimed.

Mom was baking cookies when we got home. We ate some while they were still hot. "My mother never makes cookies," Ginny said wistfully.

She made a special point of playing with Matt. I showed her his T-stool. "Here, Mattie," I said. "Show Ginny how it works."

He was pleased with the attention, so he put the stool down and sat on it. After a moment he fell over backwards, but he had never before sat on it at all. "Mom!" I cried. "Mattie sat on the stool!"

She ran in from the kitchen to see. "Oh, Mattie, you did it! You really did! I knew you could. I just knew it!" She stooped down and hugged him tight. He laughed and gurgled, and then he put the stool under himself again.

Before she went home, Ginny said, "You have a nice family. You all like each other a lot."

It seemed a funny thing for her to say, but after she left, Mom told me that Ginny's parents were getting a divorce. I was shocked. I stopped short in the middle of the floor and forgot why I had come into the kitchen. Thoughts whirled through my head. That must be why Ginny always looked so solemn these days. Maybe it even explained why she hadn't been very nice for so long.

"She's going through a lot of pain," Mom said.

"That's strange," I said thoughtfully.

"You didn't know?"

"No. I always thought everything was simple for Ginny. I didn't know she *ever* had any problems."

"There's hardly anyone in the world who doesn't have some problem or other," Mom remarked.

"Will she have to leave that big house, with the swimming pool and bunk beds?" I asked.

"I don't know."

"I *hope* she won't have to move back to Connecticut!"

"I hope not too," Mom replied. She was washing the glasses that had piled up in the sink all afternoon, and she complained, "When you kids get a drink, I *wish* you'd leave your glasses where you know whose is whose. It isn't necessary for one person to use five different glasses for five drinks of water in one hour!"

"I didn't," I replied absently.

I leaned against the refrigerator door and stared at Mom's back. "I hope you and Dad never get divorced."

"I certainly hope not too!" Mom exclaimed, drying her hands.

"You won't, will you?"

"No, I promise. We need each other too much. Think how much worse our problems would be if we didn't have each other."

"You mean with Matt?" I asked, trying to understand.

"I mean *all* the family problems that seem to go with having a handicapped child—or any other problems, for that matter."

She sat down at the kitchen table at her favorite place by the window and gazed out into the back yard. The puppy was whining to come in, but she didn't seem to hear him.

I opened the kitchen door and stooped to pat the puppy's head. "I'd rather be me than Ginny," I told Mom. "Our problems aren't as bad as hers."

"You're right," Mom said with more spirit. "I've no right to feel sorry for myself."

The puppy licked my hands, and I scooped him up into my arms. I only dimly realized how tired Mom sounded, because my mind was on Ginny and how everything had been reversed. I used to be the lonely one; now Ginny was. Life was really much more complicated than I'd realized before. It was as if Ginny had suddenly become handicapped, too. I couldn't save her from it, but perhaps I could help her through it, simply by being her friend. I would invite her over lots of times to play. At our house she seemed to cheer up a little, and I was glad.

Mom was out often these days. She spent a lot of time at Mattie's school and at a recreational center for handicapped children. She also went to a great many meetings. Sometimes Mrs. Briggs and other ladies met at our house in the evenings, and the rest of the family had to stay out of the living room then. Sometimes their discussions went on until late. I don't know what these meetings were all about, something to do with getting more programs for kids like Matt. Now that we had persuaded him to sit on the T-stool, Mom was sure he could learn more and more other things.

Two nights a week Mom went to the class about how kids learn. "I wish I had known all this when the rest of you were small," she said one night as she dressed to go.

"All of what?" I flopped across the double bed and hung my arms down the other side, near where Mom stood to comb her hair.

"How the mind and body grow and develop to-gether," she said briskly as she adjusted a bobby pin. "There's a special order to everything. It's very excit-ing. For the first time I'm getting some tools to help Matt grow up."

"Won't he just do that anyway? I mean, not like *us*, but his own way?"

"That's what I think, too," Dad said, coming out of the bathroom. "You can't force him to be something he isn't. You give him love. That's what every child needs."

I looked up at Mom. Her eyes were suddenly watery again, but she shook her head firmly. "No. Mrs. Manley was right about this. If I do everything, there's a chance. . . . I didn't see it before, but now I do." She leaned close to the mirror to put on lipstick. Dad glanced at her and frowned slightly. I don't think he liked all her new ideas.

He and I both followed her to the front door. "Just don't wear yourself out," he said uneasily as he held her coat for her. "Nothing's worth that. Take a flashlight," he added.

I noticed then that Mom was very thin. Her face looked pale, and her coat sagged off her shoulders. Her hair had some gray streaks in it, too, but there was a new light in her eyes, a new energy. She had more hope for Matt than she used to have.

"Don't you like her going to the course?" I asked Dad as he shut the front door again. He was still frowning thoughtfully.

"If it's what she wants to do, it's fine with me," he replied, but then he couldn't resist adding, "Personally, I don't think all the theories in the world are going to make much difference to Matt's life, but if it makes your mother feel better, that's all right too. I just don't like having her wander around at night." Mostly, I think, it felt strange to him not to have her there at home. Until now she had never gone anywhere without him.

Mrs. Manley, though, was pleased about the course. Mom told her all about it when she came to see us the next time. I could see Mom was enjoying their discussion more than usual, because she offered Mrs. Manley a cup of tea. Just as Mom got up to make it, Mrs. Manley said to her, "What you're learning could be important for Peter too."

"Why Peter?" I asked, leaning over the back of the couch.

She hesitated. She hadn't meant me to hear that. "Peter is younger," she explained. "Younger children tend to copy the older ones."

"Peter doesn't copy Matt," I said quickly. "It's the other way 'round," but as I said it, I remembered how Peter sometimes talked "Mattie-talk," shaping his words into Matt-like sounds.

Mrs. Manley changed the subject then; she asked about my birthday party. I slid like an otter off the back of the couch into Mom's place and told her about Matt's getting lost.

"How did you feel about that?" she asked me. She sucked the eraser on her pencil while she waited for my answer.

"I don't know. It worked out all right, I guess."

"Perhaps it was a good thing in the end," she remarked with a question in her voice. "All of you were involved together in the hunt. That made the other girls understand better how you felt. Isn't that right?"

"I guess so," I agreed. "They like me better now." Actually, the birthday party already seemed a long time ago.

"I'm so glad," she said. "You deserve to have good friends."

I blushed. I was never completely convinced by Mrs. Manley, even when she was trying hard to be nice.

"I'm a little late," she said then, "but I have something for you too." She handed me a small package wrapped in silver paper and watched me eagerly as I opened it. Inside was a bracelet with a small gold heart.

I was touched. She didn't *have* to give me a birthday present: she just did it to be nice. I felt the chain, heavy as sand in the palm of my hand, and couldn't speak. My voice stayed hidden inside me, but, looking up, I saw a smile on Mrs. Manley's face and knew she had already understood my thanks.

8

Everything finally seemed to be going well for me. I had friends at school, and I was doing better in my work as well. Then, quite suddenly, Mom got sick.

At first she pretended it was nothing serious, but we all knew she wasn't well. She often had headaches and had to lie down. Finally Dad took her to see a doctor. She didn't want to go, but he insisted. The doctor put her right into the hospital. It was a terrible shock to us all. Except for the cold she had had earlier in the year,

86

she had never been sick. Now she had jaundice. That's a liver disease that makes your skin yellow; it takes you a long time to get well.

"It's because she was run-down," Dad said. "I knew she was trying to do too much." He paced up and down the way he always does when he's upset or doesn't know what to do.

"How long will she have to stay?"

"I don't know. I don't want her coming home before she's well and then getting sick again."

"Who's going to take care of Matt and Peter?" Janet asked.

"I'll find someone."

He stayed home himself the first day, but he could hardly stand it. The house was a mess, Peter was crying, and Matt followed every step Dad took. "I'll go nuts if I have to do this for long," Dad complained as I helped him take clothes out of the dryer. "I was supposed to go to Chicago in a couple of days, too. Now I can't."

He put an ad in the newspaper for someone to help, and a few people called to ask about it, but when he explained about Matt, no one wanted the job. Mrs.

Manley tried to find someone, too, but no one worked out.

Mom had always held everything together at home. Now she wasn't here. There was a lot of confusion in our house about who should do what.

Finally Mrs. Briggs came to our rescue. She offered to take Peter to nursery school and to meet Matt's bus when he came home from school. She would keep both boys until Mary and I were there. She even found other neighbors to fill in on days when she was working or had to be somewhere else. Mrs. Briggs was just wonderful!

Still, we had to cope for ourselves before school and again later in the day. Janet's bus leaves very early in the morning, so Mary and I dressed Matt and Peter for school. The first day Matt took advantage of us like anything. He giggled and went all limp so that the game of getting dressed would last longer. Finally Mary lost her temper. "Hurry up, Matt," she said. "I can't spend all day." Then he cooperated while she brushed his teeth, letting her guide the brush, clamped tight in his own fist, around his mouth.

At last he was ready. We were both dreading the bus

scene. "I always thought it was a mistake for Mom to drive him to school," Mary complained. "She should have stood firm the very first time."

Matt knew exactly where we were going. In the middle of the sidewalk, he balked. His body went stiff, and he braced his feet against a ridge in the concrete pavement. We pulled and shoved, but we couldn't budge him. He jabbered Mattie-talk, none of which was clear except the word "no."

"Come on, Matt," Mary pleaded. "Your friend Jim's up there at the corner. Don't you want to see Jim?"

Matt shook his head.

"*We're* going to school in a minute," Mary went on. "We're going on *our* school bus. There's *your* bus coming. You wouldn't want to miss school. School's fun."

Still Mattie's body was rigid, like a board.

"Damn it," Mary said, "you *have* to, that's all!"

With a burst of strength she grabbed him around the middle, hoisted him off the ground, and began to stumble toward the bus stop. I stared at her with admiration. Even Janet and I together hadn't handled him so well that day at the park. Mattie sobbed into Mary's neck and kicked at the air behind her back, but she got him to the bus, while I followed uselessly behind her. The driver took Mattie from her arms and strapped him onto a seat. Then the doors of the bus folded shut over Matt's cries of protest. The bus groaned a little and then crept away.

"That was awful," Mary said, wiping the sweat off her forehead. "I'm exhausted. Think it will be like that every day?"

"Maybe not," I said hopefully. "You handled him really well."

"Thanks," she said. "The worst part is, I understand how he feels. I hate the bus ride myself. The bus fumes smell awful, the motion makes me carsick, and the noise gives me a headache. We've got to hurry now, though, or we'll miss ours."

After school we picked Matt and Peter up at the Briggses' house. Matt was very glad to see us. Mrs. Briggs said he had spent the whole day looking for Mom. He positively clung to Mary the rest of the afternoon. Right away he latched onto her as a substitute for Mom.

At home we discovered that no one had thawed hamburger for supper and that the dog food had run out. Peter began to fuss because he wanted apple juice, and there was only orange juice in the refrigerator. The living-room floor was even more cluttered than usual, and it seemed as if a week's laundry had piled up in one day. I was too tired to solve any of these problems; I waited for Mary to do something about them.

Actually, we all depended on Mary in a way. Even Dad asked her advice about things. Mary was the practical one in the family, and she could usually figure out what to do. She also liked to cook, so it was natural for her to take charge of the meals. Janet was too late getting home to be much help.

Dad made the rule that anyone who complained about the food would have to cook the next time, so no one told Mary that her hamburgers were overdone or that we were sick of baked potatoes. Besides, her experiments were worse. Once Dad forgot his own rule and told Mary that her tapioca pudding would be better not quite so thick, but when she made it again the next night, he told her it was delicious! Then she was satisfied, and we didn't get it again.

"I don't see why Janet can't come home early *some* days," Mary complained once. "I can't do *everything*."

"I get home as soon as I can," Janet argued. "I can't come before the bus does. As it is, I haven't been to a glee club practice all week, and I missed a student council meeting."

"Glee club practice!" Mary cried. "Isn't that too bad! Sarah and I haven't gotten out for *anything*. I'm missing a soccer game on Friday, and it's our most important game," she added.

"Girls, girls," Dad said, stepping between them. "Let's try to work this out."

"How?" Mary demanded, glaring at Dad. Indeed, there was no simple solution.

"All right," Janet offered, "I'll hitchhike home early."

"No," Dad said. "*That* I won't have."

Mary began to get bossy. She said if she did the cooking, I should wash the dishes. When Mom was there, Mary and Janet and I all took turns, with one of us washing and one drying, so I thought it should still work the same way, but Dad took Mary's side.

"What about Janet?" I demanded.

"Janet can put the boys to bed," Mary declared, so I was stuck with the dishes. They seemed endless. The sink was already full before we even ate dinner. Now I saw what Mom meant about hundreds of juice and water glasses.

I didn't like having Mary tell me to put away my own laundry or pick up my pajamas. I could figure those things out for myself; I just never seemed to get around to doing them soon enough to suit Mary. I resented her taking over for Mom, and I didn't realize how hard it was for her.

Mattie never gave Mary a moment's rest. He wanted to hold her hand or sit in her lap all the time. He followed every step she took around the house, and he cried when she put him on the bus in the morning. He whimpered even when she put him in the playpen, and Mary had to be the one to kiss him good night.

I felt very sorry for Mattie, because he didn't understand where Mom had gone. I could see that he was miserable, and I tried to cheer him up by handing him toys to throw and tumbling with him on the floor, but nothing seemed to distract him. Even when I cuddled him, he looked for Mary. I couldn't help being jealous. Deep down, though, in view of the way I had treated him recently, I thought his choice seemed natural enough.

~9

When Mom finally came home, we celebrated with roast beef for dinner. We were all *so* happy she was better. "We missed you like anything," I told her.

"I missed you too," she said, hugging us all together in one big clump.

She was still very thin and weak, though, and her skin still had that yellow look. She wasn't allowed to work. She had to stay quiet, and we weren't to make any noise. I didn't understand very well what was wrong, but I knew it would take a long time for her to be her old self again.

We all thought the problems would go away now that Mom was home again, but they didn't. Peter, for instance, was in a new, bad phase. He kept having temper tantrums and fighting with Matt. Mom said he needed more attention, but she didn't have the energy to give it to him. We girls still had to do all the cleaning up and baby-sit after school. I hardly saw Ginny, and that was hard on me. Ginny needed me, and I wanted to be with her. Then, too, Dad was away a lot again. Altogether, it was a bad time.

Then, without consulting the rest of us, Mom and Dad decided to send Mattie away. It happened right after one of Dad's longer trips.

"How can you do that?" I cried when they told us. "Don't you love him any more?" I thought of all the times I had wished Matt away, but now I felt sick inside.

"Of course we do," Mom said. "It's not anything final, and he can come home for visits. It just seems best for right now, till I'm back on my feet."

"Where will he go?" Mary asked.

"It's a foster home not very far from here," Dad said. "We were lucky to get a place. It's run by a lady named Mrs. Bronson. She has five or six children there in all."

"Like Mattie?"

"Some of them are older," Dad replied.

"But he'll miss us terribly," I said. "Oh, terribly. He was miserable when Mom was gone. He'll never understand."

Mom looked very pained.

"And why Mattie?" I went on. "Peter's more trouble, really. He starts all the fights. Why not *me?*"

Dad said slowly, "There may be a time when Matt has to live away from home. Someday he'll need friends like himself. When he's older, it might be better for him to live with them. Or if something happened to us. . . . This is a chance for Matt to get used to being away from us."

"But it's not fair."

There were tears in Mom's eyes. She said, "Now that I'm sick, I can't do what he needs. I can't work with him enough. I can't even finish my course. He needs so much special training. I'm just beginning to learn how to help. When I'm well, I can do it, but now I can't."

"Oh, Mom."

"Sometimes you show your love more by doing what's hard."

I remembered the day when Mom had been crying after Mrs. Manley's visit. It came to me in a flash that they must have discussed this then. Only such a drastic suggestion would upset Mom that much. Mom had told me then that Mrs. Manley's solution was not to deal with life at all. I should have understood then, but I didn't.

"Is this what Mrs. Manley wanted?" I asked now.

"No, it is our own decision," Mom told me in a trembling voice. "It's true that I've discussed it with her from time to time. When you were so unhappy, she asked me to consider it as a possible option. That shocked me then. I didn't see that it solved anything. You had to learn that Mattie was part of life. We all start out wanting life to be perfect, and it never is. Sometimes it's pretty hard to accept *how* imperfect it can be."

"Then why?" I slipped my hand into hers and searched her eyes for an answer.

"Our problems are different now. I'm thinking of Matt, not you." But *I* didn't understand how this could possibly be for Matt's good.

Matt was already in bed. He didn't know anything about it yet. In spite of what Mom had said, I couldn't get over it. I went into the kitchen. High in a cupboard I found a bag of marshmallows Mom was saving for a picnic. Matt loves marshmallows more than anything.

I slipped into Matt's room without turning on the light. He sat up in the dark and poked at my face through the bars of the crib. I leaned over and kissed his face all over.

I opened the bag of marshmallows and put one in his hand. He squeezed it and passed it to the other hand and squeezed it again. Then he shoved it all into his mouth. Saliva ran down his chin because his mouth was so full.

I wiped his mouth with the corner of the sheet. Even in the dark I knew he was smiling. He reached for more. I gave him another. "That's enough, Mattie," I said, but he grabbed the bar of the crib and shook the whole bed. Matt is strong. I was afraid he would tip the bed over or Mom would hear, so I gave him some more. Finally he had eaten the whole bag of marshmallows.

In the night Mattie was sick. Mom and Dad took turns getting up with him. They ran out of sheets for the crib, so Mom had to do a load of laundry in the middle of the night.

I hid the marshmallow bag in the bottom of the trash, but I felt sick too. The last thing I meant to do was to hurt Matt. I wanted him to remember me as his friend. Also, I knew Mom needed all the sleep she could get. After a day of being miserable, I confessed. I expected to be punished, but Mom just shook her head sadly, and that was worse. "That's why it's best for him to go away for a while. It's a terrible responsibility for all of us here at home. I thought you had gotten past your crisis over Mattie, but perhaps all of us just need a little time."

10

At first after Matt left, I felt wonderfully free. When I walked down the street or went to school, I felt like saying, "Look at me, everybody. There's nothing different about me now. I'm exactly like you."

At home everything was suddenly easy. We all laughed a lot more than we used to. In the evenings we played card games together or sometimes Scrabble. Even Dad played instead of reading his newspapers or watching TV.

There wasn't nearly as much work. Peter suddenly toilet-trained himself. He just stopped wetting. That meant much less laundry, which was great for Mary and me, because we still had to take turns running the machine and sorting the clean clothes.

Peter had no one to fight with any more, and I only had to tell him things once. With Matt, you have to repeat everything over and over. Besides, lots of people invited Peter over to play with their kids, now that it was just him and not Matt too.

One night, Dad took the whole family to a fancy Chinese restaurant. Even Peter came. We hadn't done anything like that since Matt was a baby.

Mary and I put on long dresses instead of our usual jeans, and tied our hair back with scarves, the way Janet does when she goes out. We were very excited.

Dad was in high spirits. "I'm particularly fond of Chinese food," he said as he drove us toward the center of San Jose. "It's one of the good things out here. We've hardly begun to take advantage of what California has to offer."

"I'd like to go to the beach sometimes," I said. "And Yosemite."

"Why not?" Dad replied.

The restaurant was rather dark and very elegant. We were seated at a big round table with a white tablecloth and linen napkins. Peter had his own special high chair pulled up to the table. With awe, I opened the large, red-covered menu and read down pages and pages of exotic dishes. Finally each of us chose one dish, to be shared by all.

Dad showed us how to hold our chopsticks, and we had a good laugh over our fumblings. A fat shrimp, covered with red, spicy sauce, escaped from me and skidded onto the tablecloth. "Oh, dear," I exclaimed, "I'm just like Mattie."

"Never mind," Mom said quickly. "They'll wash the cloth afterwards anyway. Have you tried the beef dish yet? It's delicious!"

I turned the lazy Susan slowly around, admiring all the different colorful piles of food, trying to decide what to take. Once, another image of Matt came to my mind. He would have loved the lazy Susan! Dishes would have flown off in every direction as he spun it. Then I quickly thought of something else. Tonight we were free from any disaster like that. No one even mentioned Matt again. We were too busy enjoying ourselves even to think of him.

Ginny came over often after school these days. We went to the park or rode bikes together whenever we felt like it. We talked about everything that had ever happened to us. She told me now about her parents getting divorced and how sad it made her because she loved them both. She was working it through, though. "It's easier, in a way, to be with just one of them at a time," she concluded.

"Like it's easier for me without Mattie."

She surprised me by replying, "I kind of miss him, now that I know him." Of course, she didn't have to be with him all the time.

I didn't realize that *I* missed him at all until we went to see him at his foster home. I was nervous about going. I didn't know what to expect. We got out of the car in front of a big old house with a covered porch and fancy carving all over it. It reminded me of a birthday cake. We all stood very still while we waited for someone to answer the bell. Then Mrs. Bronson came. She was a short, round lady with a kind face. She took us into the living room, where there was a great big round table and lots of indoor plants.

Mattie was playing on the floor with a girl who was about my size. They were scratching each other's backs. He looked confused when he saw us, as if he didn't know for sure who we were.

"Mattie, it's me," I said, putting my arms around him. Then he pulled my hair, and I knew he remembered.

Mary gave him some chocolate. Soon his hands and face were brown and sticky. We all smiled at him. He was so pleased. "All for you, Mattie," Mary said.

An older boy came in and sat down to tie his shoe. It took him a long time, but at last he did it. Mom and I exchanged a look. "Do you think Matt will ever learn to do that?" I asked.

"Of course he will," Mom said.

"Can he come home with us now?"

"Not today," Dad said, taking my hand.

"It's better to wait," Mrs. Bronson explained, "until he's fully adjusted. He's doing very well," she added, patting him on the head. She held one of his hands as we were leaving and told him to wave good-by. He copied her waving, but there was a blank look in his eyes.

"I feel so sad for Mattie," I said as we were driving home. Everybody was being very quiet.

"Mrs. Bronson's kind," Mom said, but there was a quiver in her voice.

"He misses us. I know he misses us."

"It takes time," Mom said. "We mustn't worry too much."

"You're getting better," I said. "Aren't you well enough yet?"

"I want your mother to have a real rest," Dad replied. "It's better for us all."

I wasn't sure any more. I felt anxious. Maybe they didn't mean for him ever to come home. They had promised to let me go with Ginny to the Y camp next summer. I had wanted to go very much. Now I felt uneasy about that. Would they be glad to get rid of me too?

"I'd rather have Matt than go to camp," I said finally.

"You do have Matt. You'll always have Matt," Dad told me firmly, "and camp will be lots of fun. I wouldn't mind going myself."

We went to see Matt again the next weekend. This time we found him playing in a sandbox in the back yard. "Hi, Mattie," I cried, rushing toward him. He laughed and threw sand at me. "Hey, you quit that, Mattie!" We all began to dig with him.

"We have a new swing," I told him. "A basket swing. When you come home, you can try it. It's wonderful. You can curl up in it and close your eyes and pretend you're riding over big ocean waves."

"Matt's never seen big ocean waves," Mary said.

"Spacecraft," Peter said.

"Sure—it can be a spacecraft too," I agreed. "You can pretend you're tumbling all different ways through space."

"*I* feel like a bird when I swing," Janet said.

Matt opened his wide, wide smile and spread out his arms like a bird. "He understood," Janet said.

"Of course he understood," I told her. "Matt understands much more than you ever think."

An older boy, with Matt's same wide-open smile, came over to the sandbox. He walked in that same awkward way Matt walks. Matt saw him and laughed. He threw sand at him, the way he did at me.

"This is Leo," Mrs. Bronson said. "Leo, say hello."

"What's your name?" Leo asked, as if his mouth were full of gum. He sounded like Matt.

"Sarah."

"Hello, Sarah. I'm Leo. You're a nice girl, Sarah. I like you."

Suddenly Leo plunged forward and hugged me tight. I pulled back, scared.

"No, Leo," Mrs. Bronson said. "You don't know Sarah, so you mustn't hug her. Now shake hands nicely."

He shook hands then, and his hand was limp and wobbly. I felt just the way Ginny did when she first met Mattie—all tight inside and uncomfortable. Then Leo turned and walked over to Matt. He ruffled Matt's hair and said, "Matt my friend." Matt looked up at him and waved.

"At home," Dad whispered, "Matt never had any friends."

"He had me," I reminded him.

"You are very special to Matt, but he needs friends as well as sisters. Everyone does."

I nodded, thinking of Ginny.

"We should go," Dad said, "while Matt is playing with his friend."

Matt saw us wave. Suddenly he pulled himself to his feet and threw himself toward Mom. Before she could move, he wrapped his arms tightly around her leg, twisting her skirt. She leaned down to untangle herself, but he held on like a mussel on a rock. She brushed the hair back from his face and said, "It's all right, Mattie. We won't go yet. Please let go. You're hurting my leg." Still, he wouldn't let go.

Dad pulled Matt's arm loose. He picked Mattie up, but Matt kicked wildly and flung his body out into the air, reaching for Mom. His face was bright red, as shiny as an apple. Tears streamed over his round cheeks. Nobody can look sadder than Mattie.

"I'll take him," Mom said. She sat down on a bench and took him in her lap. He clutched her around the neck and sobbed. She kissed his wet face and held him very safely until he was quiet and his smile came out again, like sunshine after a hard rain.

11

At home we had a long, troubled discussion about Matt. We had just finished a rather silent meal and were still gathered around the dinner table. "Even if I'm not strong yet we can't leave him," Mom said suddenly. "I never did feel sure. Now I know it isn't right."

Dad said, "We knew it would be hard. We haven't given it a very long try."

"What does that mean—*try*?" I asked.

"Nothing's ever definite," Dad said.

"You mean—you might just leave him there?" I was horrified.

"It would be a possibility—but only if it seemed to be working out for the best."

"It's not, though. Obviously, it's not."

"The older he gets, the harder it will be for him to leave us."

"That's the same argument we heard when he was born," Mom sighed. "I didn't buy it then, and I still don't."

"In the long run," Dad said, "he'll be happier if he isn't judged by the standards of the outside world."

"He's part of the world," Mom said, "and I believe he can learn to live in it."

"We don't really know what he can learn or what's best for him," Dad said, rolling his napkin.

"He's our brother," Janet said thoughtfully. I looked at her, and then I looked at Mom and nodded.

"No one there loves him," I said. "They're nice, but they don't love him. Only we can do that."

"That's true," Dad said. He reached across the corner of the table and covered my hand with his. "I had hoped we might have a real vacation together this summer, perhaps at the beach, where your mother could get her health back."

There was a pause. I thought about how nice this would be.

Janet said, "You know that girl I met whose twelve-year-old brother is Downs? They've put him into an institution now. Her family couldn't handle it any more. She thinks it was the right thing, but the way she talks about it all the time, she must not feel too sure."

Dad said, "None of us can ever be sure we're doing the best thing for our children. There is no right or wrong about it." He pushed his chair back from the table and crossed his legs.

"We do what feels right at the time," Mom added. "That's all. It might be the opposite for someone else. It took courage to do what they did."

"In our case," Dad said, "it doesn't have to be a final decision either way. We might all change our minds later on. We don't know what the problems will be when he's older."

"Or the joys," Mom added. "When Matt was born, I never dreamed of the joys. He has heightened my life, so that everything means more."

"Perhaps that's because we can't see ahead," Dad mused. "We live from day to day."

No one spoke for a moment. Then Janet said quietly, "It has been easier without him, but in spite of everything, I think Matt should come home. He tried to tell us."

"Me too," I said quickly.

"You're sure, Sarah?" Dad asked.

I nodded.

"We must make the decision together. It must be right for us all. How do you feel, Mary?"

"I don't know," Mary murmured, not looking at anyone. "We've all been much *gayer* lately. More like the way we used to be. . . . You've spent more time with us, playing games and things. . . . We could never have gone to that nice restaurant with Mattie." She paused, biting her lip. Finally she said apologetically, "I think he should stay where he is. I *do* love him, but I don't want him *here*." I was shocked. I'd never known she felt that way.

Tears gushed up in Mary's eyes. She wiped her nose on the back of her arm.

"Here," Mom said. "Here's a Kleenex."

Dad said in a disconcerted voice, "It's important to be honest. That's what I asked you to be. We all appreciate, Mary, how much of the load you carried while your mother was sick."

At that Mary broke down again. She cried into the Kleenex. Mom moved her chair closer to Mary's and slid her arm around Mary's shoulder. None of us spoke. I could see Mary needed a good cry. At last she blew her nose on another Kleenex and said, "I feel better now."

"There are some other factors you should know," Dad said carefully. "One is the expense. We can't afford to leave Matt where he is without help. Right now the state is paying most of the cost, but these state funds may be cut off any time."

"How can they do that?" I asked soberly.

"All too easily," Dad replied. "It's a question of politics. Right now the state budget is all up in the air. They're arguing over whether the money should go to foster homes or state hospitals. It's a mess. Nobody knows how much there will be for anything."

"How depressing," Janet said, twisting her ponytail.

"There's another problem, too," Dad went on. "The people who live around Mrs. Bronson's house are trying to shut it down."

"Shut it down?" I repeated. "How?"

"They've signed a petition to the county. They claim it violates the zoning laws, and that, moreover, the building isn't up to code."

"What does that mean?"

"It's an old building. They claim if there was a fire. . ."

"How horrible!" Mary cried.

"But that's not the real point," Dad said hastily. "The real point is that people don't like to see handicapped kids wandering around. It reminds them that it might have happened to them just as well. People don't want to know about other people's problems."

"That's just as bad," Mary said angrily. "It isn't fair."

"No, it isn't," Dad agreed, playing with his napkin ring, "but that's human nature, I'm afraid. That's where it is."

Mary's cheeks were dry now. Her eyes flashed. "I've

changed my mind," she announced, sitting up very straight.

"I think Mrs. Bronson will probably win her case with the county," Dad said, "and even if she doesn't, there are other foster homes. We haven't explored all the options."

"He can't keep moving," Mary said. "He should come home. It wasn't supposed to be forever. I was just thinking of myself."

"You're important, too," Mom said.

"I want everyone to be very, very sure," Dad said, looking from one of us to another. "We should give ourselves plenty of time."

"I'm sure now," Mary insisted. "I mean, I guess I can stand its being hard."

"I'd like Mary to have her ballet lessons," Mom put in. "She's wanted them for so long. If Matt does come home, couldn't we use the money we save for that?"

"Excellent idea," Dad agreed. "You need to get out more, too. I'd like to hire someone one day a week so that you can do anything you want. Take that pottery class you used to talk about. Something like that."

Mom smiled. "That would be nice, but we'll see.

First, I want to finish the course I started before I was sick."

She got up and began to clear the dinner table. "Sit down," Dad ordered. "The girls can do that."

"What about Peter?" I asked as I got up. "He's too young to vote."

"That's true," Dad said, tipping back his chair.

Janet stopped on her way to the kitchen. She turned around with her hands full of dishes and told Dad, "He's changed a lot since Matt went away. For him, it's probably better this way. His speech has improved a whole lot."

"Peter's always had Matt here," I said. "It's just normal for him. Remember what you told me? You said we all grew up faster because of Matt. Well, I hadn't done it then. It took me a while, but I made it. Peter will too. He just needs a little time."

"I love you all for this," Mom said, giving in to her tears. "I can't sort out the arguments any more. For me, it's very simple. I miss him too much. Maybe the balance will be different later on, but I'm not ready to give him up so soon. Now you've given me one more gift of joy."

So we brought Matt home. Somehow he knew that this was why we had come back. He walked in a circle, holding onto Mary and then Janet and then me. Finally he came to Dad and grabbed one finger of his hand. He looked up with his wide smile and jerked at Dad. He began to march, in his toy-soldier march, across the lawn toward our car.

"He knows he's coming home," I cried. "Oh, Mattie!"

After supper we all played with him on the floor. We had a pillow fight, and Mattie loved that. He laughed and threw pillows everywhere. Even Mom, who had always forbidden pillow fights, joined in. We all threw our pillows at her at once, and she rolled on the floor with Mattie and laughed.

"Mattie always loved to play like this," I said. "Look how happy he is."

"I'm afraid he'll think pillows are for throwing all the time," Mom said.

"Never mind," Dad told her. "He's right, in a way. All his life he's been trying to teach us how to play. We just haven't understood what he meant. Now we do a little better."

"Just go on laughing that way forever," I begged Mom.

She did a surprising thing. She lay down on the floor and held Peter on her feet in a flying angel. "If you'll all help me," she promised. "Forever and ever."

At once Mattie scrambled onto her. "Wait, Matt," she pleaded, laughing. "It's not your turn." But Mattie couldn't wait. He tugged at Mom's legs until Peter toppled over him. Matt wanted to be an angel, too.

∽ Anne Norris Baldwin

grew up in Pennsylvania. She attended Smith College
and went on to Harvard, where she received a Ph.D. in
biochemistry. She has contributed articles to scientific
journals and has written five books for children.

The idea for this book began several years ago while
Mrs. Baldwin and her husband were on sabbatical leave
in Paris. In a local park she spent many hours observing
a child with Down's syndrome. The experience stayed
with her and eventually grew into an idea for a book.

Mrs. Baldwin now lives in California with her husband and two sons. *A Little Time* is her first book for
Viking.